# #3:
# The Legend of Skull Cliff

by Kristiana Gregory
illustrated by Cody Rutty

THE LEGEND OF SKULL CLIFF is a work of fiction with characters and events from the author's imagination.

Dedicated to the Coen cousins: William, Nic, Cari Lynn, James, Woodrow and Ashley.

# Chapters

# 1
# The Cliff

*T*en-year-old David Bridger stood near the edge of Skull Cliff, looking out at the vast lake and the distant range of mountains. It was windy this high up. He brushed his blond hair from his eyes. Then he kicked some gravel to see how far it would fly before dropping from sight. As usual, his socks were mismatched: one striped, one plain.

"Hey, Jeff," he said to his older brother. "What d'you think would happen if we slipped?"

"The cold water would knock us out," Jeff answered, pulling David away from the railing. He was twelve and cautious about such things. He and his brother wore T-shirts. Jeff's still had a crease from where it had been neatly folded in his drawer, but David's was inside out because he often dressed in a hurry.

"Remember those boys Dad told us about?" asked Jeff. "From when he was a kid?"

"Sorta."

"Well, they were goofing around up here and fell," Jeff reminded him. "Even though they knew how to swim, they sank and never came up."

David shivered. It was just another spooky story about Skull Cliff. "Oh ... yeah ... I remember now. Then it's a good thing the dogs are safe at home. Except for you-know-who." He glanced at their cousin Claire, who held a white poodle in her arms.

"Yum-Yum is perfectly safe. Don't worry," she replied, showing the sparkly pink leash wrapped around her hand. Claire Posey was nine. Her curly red hair was held back with a barrette that matched Yum-Yum's yellow collar. A pair of binoculars hung around Claire's neck. With her free hand she looked through them, adjusting the focus with a practiced thumb.

"I hope no one can see our fort from here," she said.

The brothers took their binoculars out of their backpacks. They scanned the lake, with its many small islands, and also Grizzly Paw Wilderness—a remote stretch of land that surrounded the shoreline. On the far southern shore, the cousins saw their log homes and the beach where their families' boats were docked.

Lost Island was hidden in the farthest northern inlet. Just this summer, their parents had allowed them to explore it for the first time. Their secret clubhouse was on this forested isle. They had made the trip that morning to make sure no one could see their fort from the top of Skull Cliff.

"We're in luck," Jeff said. "No one will ever guess that tall tree is our lookout tower. You can't even see the platform."

A shout drew their attention to the dirt road leading up to the cliff.

"Uh-oh," said Claire. "Here they come. No more peace and quiet."

A small blue bus was unloading by the picnic area. Painted on its side was camp whispering pines, showing a log cabin with pine trees. Already, kids chased one another around clumps of sagebrush and yelled at the top of their lungs. Two boys began sword fighting with twigs.

One of the counselors blew his whistle. He held a clipboard and wore a T-shirt with a logo that matched the bus's. "People!" he called. "It's ten o'clock, so we'll start the hike in fifteen minutes. Since this is our third hike this week, you should remember the rules."

He now shouted to be heard. "Stay on the trail, people! Don't pick any wildflowers! Do not tease the chipmunks! And no throwing pinecones like last time! You could poke someone's eye out!"

Jeff and David gave each other satisfied looks. They knew all this. Their father had been a forest ranger before he died last winter and he had taught them well. He had loved showing city kids the mountains and how to respect nature. In fact, his love for the wilderness had begun when he himself was a child at Camp Whispering Pines. Jeff had his dad's brown hair and deep brown eyes.

After some moments of watching the campers, Jeff suddenly craned his neck, looking behind and around him. "Where's Claire?" His voice was urgent. "She never goes anywhere without telling us."

"Uh ... don't know. She was right here."

"Claire!" they called, trying to spot their cousin among the crowd.

Knowing the history of the cliff, the boys grew nervous when they didn't see her. They turned toward the overhang. Without saying anything, they crept forward. Once at the railing, they peered over the rim, down to the blue lake. David's stomach twirled from the dizzying height. Jeff no longer felt brave. With their binoculars, they searched the water, hoping Claire and her little white poodle had not slipped from the edge.

"She's always so careful," Jeff said. "But what if she fell?"

"We better call for help!" David unhooked his walkie- talkie from his belt.

"What are you guys doing?" came a voice behind them. The brothers whipped around. "Claire!" they cried.

"Hey," she said, uncertain why they were so excited to see her. "You won't believe this kid named Willie, from Whispering Pines," she said. "He wants to buy Yum-Yum because he's lonesome for his dog at home. He tried to give me a fifty-dollar bill."

"That's crazy!" David exclaimed, still relieved to see that Claire was safe.

Claire shrugged her shoulders. "I know. The kid claims camp is boring, so he's going to make some fun of his own."

"That doesn't sound good," Jeff said. As the oldest, most responsible cousin, he now worried. Jeff returned his gaze to the icy water beneath Skull Cliff, then to the expanse of wilderness beyond the

9

lake. His dad had taught him that nature provided all the excitement a kid could need—and sometimes more.

# 2
# Rich Kid

Skull Cliff was popular with tourists because of the magnificent view of the mountains. There was a picnic area near a stream and campsites tucked among the pine trees. During summer, a small shuttle bus drove up the hill every hour from town, so fewer cars cluttered the area with noise and fumes. Not only did visitors arrive with lunch and cameras, they came with their cell phones. The high elevation made reception possible, unlike on the lake.

While the cousins drank from their canteens, a twelve- year-old boy approached them. He wore a brown button-down shirt with shorts and flip-flops. His dark hair was combed with gel.

Claire sighed when she saw him. "I told you already, Willie. My dog is not for sale."

"Okay, okay. Just thought I'd ask one more time." Hands in his pockets, he regarded David's untidy shirt and socks. "Dude, you look like a bum."

The younger boy ignored the insult. "What would you do with a dog, anyway?" David asked. "Camp is only one week long."

"Well, I get to stay till the end of August," the camper bragged. "My parents are traveling overseas, so this is my fourth week here."

Jeff thought about what Willie said. "Why didn't you go to a horse ranch that lasted all summer? There are lots of them in the West."

"Ah, my dad went here when he was my age," the boy answered.

"That's kinda nice," David said, thinking about his own father.

"Well, yeah. Except these little nature hikes and campfire sing-alongs are getting old. I need more action, more excitement."

The brothers glanced at Claire, and she gave them an I- told-you-so look.

"Really, I should be a junior counselor. I could lead the hikes, I've been on them so many times," the boy continued. "I could show the new kids a thing or two. Watch, someday people will be proud of Willie Stamper. That's me."

"What do you mean?" Jeff asked. But he was interrupted by the loud music from a cell phone in Willie's daypack.

Willie answered the call, turning his back on the cousins. They couldn't hear his conversation except that he spoke politely and kept saying, "Okay, Mom." Finally, he snapped his phone shut with a flick of his wrist.

"That was one of my buddies," Willie said to them. "We call each other every day."

Claire exchanged looks with Jeff and David.

"What? You don't believe me?" Willie glared at the cousins.

Hugging Yum-Yum to her chest, Claire said, "I hope you don't do anything dangerous."

"Sure thing, Miss Bossy."

"I'm serious," she said. "It's not as safe out here as it looks. There are grizzlies."

"Mind your own business, why don't you!"

"Come on, guys," Jeff said, leading Claire and David away. He didn't like arguments. "We're supposed to meet Mom for lunch in ten minutes."

The cousins waited for the next shuttle. A lady standing nearby was talking on her cell phone in a low voice. She wore dark sunglasses.

" ... spoiled rich kids," she said. " ... I'll teach them a lesson they won't soon forget."

Claire and the brothers tried to hear more, but suddenly the woman put her phone in her purse. She glanced behind her, then hurried away.

"Wonder what that was about," the kids whispered to one another.

The bus wound its way down the hill into the town of Cabin Creek. When it stopped at the animal hospital, the cousins got out. They had parked their bikes here this morning after riding from home.

Dr. Daisy Bridger was just changing out of her white coat for lunch. She was the town's veterinarian and the boys' mother. She had the same blue eyes and blond hair as David. Her long braid was tied with string.

"I'm glad to see you," she said with a smile. Carrying a picnic basket, she led them to a shaded courtyard, which had a view of Main Street. She spread sandwiches, potato chips, and pickles onto a table. She set out a pitcher of apple juice.

"And how's your day so far?" she asked the children, passing them each a cup of juice.

They discussed their morning while eating lunch in the shade. It was peaceful until a white pickup truck zoomed down Main Street. It barreled from Skull Cliff Road out of town. The female driver wore sunglasses, and a boy sat in the backseat. His dark hair was neatly combed and he wore a brown collared shirt. The boy was crying and shaking his head as if shouting. Then, in a cloud of dust, the truck was gone.

Mom looked at her watch. "That driver must be running late, like my one o'clock appointment. Well, since Fluffy and her owner aren't here yet, I'll join you kids for dessert." She opened a box of cookies to pass around.

Twenty minutes later, a lady parked her car at the curb and hurried onto the sidewalk with a carrying case. Inside was a yowling cat. The woman's face was flushed.

"Oh, Dr. Bridger," she said, out of breath. "I'm sorry I'm late, but did you hear the dreadful news from Skull Cliff?"

"What? What?" they asked.

"One of the campers from Whispering Pines has vanished. When the counselors did roll call, he was nowhere to be found. I was up there having a picnic with my sister, and we had to wait for the police to question us before we could leave."

"Oh, dear," Mom said.

The cousins looked at one another, wondering. "Did you hear who it was?" Jeff asked.

"Mm. I don't remember the name," the woman answered. "At first, everyone worried he fell off the cliff. You know how kids push and shove. And then someone said they had seen a bear. But then a counselor found a note in the brush, all crumpled up. It mentions money and that a child will die. People think it's a demand for ransom."

"My heavens," said Mom. "A kidnapping, here in Cabin Creek? It's such a small town."

"Exactly," said the woman. "My sister and I are worried sick that more children are in danger."

# 3
# Kidnapped

*A*fter Fluffy's owner went into the animal clinic, Claire said, "I knew something bad might happen."

"What do you mean, honey?" asked Mom.

"Aunt Daisy, remember that boy we told you about, who tried to buy Yum-Yum? He was showing off like he knows everything about nature, but he was wearing flip- flops to go on a hike."

"So?"

"Well, the trails are full of cactus and sharp stones," Claire replied. "He'll cut his feet."

Jeff said, "If the kid's so smart, why didn't he wear sneakers or hiking boots?"

"Yeah," David agreed, taking his sketch pad from his pack. He was in the habit of drawing interesting things to look at later. As he began sketching the truck from memory, he added, "And that kid's hair gel smelled like bubblegum. If a bear tries to sniff him, he could get eaten."

Dr. Bridger closed the box of cookies and returned it to her picnic basket. "Children, how do you know the missing boy is the camper you met? And what does any of this have to do with being kidnapped?"

The cousins were quiet for a moment. Then Claire answered, "Willie   Stamper is a loudmouth. Maybe someone saw him with  that  fifty-dollar bill and figured he's rich. The kid in that  truck looked like him—remember, he was crying or something? What if the driver stole him and that's why she was going so fast?"

"This certainly is upsetting," said Mom. "Be careful not to jump to conclusions, though."

Jeff wadded up their sandwich wrappers and tossed them into a trashcan. "Mom, may I use the phone in your office?  I think  we  should  tell the police  about  that  white pickup."

"Of course, dear.  But don't get too distracted. Remember, Ariel will be here before sunset to take you all camping.  You need to get your sleeping bags and tent."

"Be right back." Jeff went inside. Through the open window, the others heard him saying, "Yes ... okay ... thank you very much."

The older boy  returned  to  the  courtyard. "Guess  what, guys?  Bad news.  We were right. Willie Stamper is missing."


*A* shortcut from town wove through the woods.  The cousins pedaled home along a trail that skirted the lake, Yum-Yum riding in Claire's basket.  For the moment, they didn't think about  the  lost  boy.  They were  excited that  their  family  friend, Ariel, was

17

taking them camping again—three nights up near Skull
Cliff. She was a college student who spent summers
working with Mom in the animal hospital.

The cousins' cabins were on the remote shore that
faced Lost Island. A creek with a wooden
footbridge separated the two properties. They
dropped their bikes on the grass and ran up the porch
steps to let out the dogs.

Jeff looked up at the blue sky. "Sun's still
overhead," he observed. "We have all afternoon."

"So let's go to
the fort!" Claire
cried.

"I'll get the
life vests!"
shouted David,
already headed for
the dock.

Yum-Yum
raced along the
beach with
Rascal—a black
Scottish terrier—
while the boys
helped Tessie into
the canoe. She was
an old yellow Lab
and had a little trouble climbing into the boat, but she
was good about sitting still for the ride across the lake.

Soon the three children and their dogs had reached the island's quiet cove. A path through the trees led them to Fort Grizzly Paw—their name for the abandoned hunter's cabin with a missing wall. To fix the place up, they had filled the empty space with a little log fence and gate. Then they had nailed a tarp on the roof to keep out the rain because a pine tree was growing straight up through the rafters. From its lower branches, the cousins had hung ropes, canteens, spare sweatshirts, sneakers, and other gear. Shelves framed the stone fireplace with dishes and a frying pan, in case they wanted to cook.

"Nothing's missing," they agreed after their usual inspection.

So far, no one else had discovered the secret hideaway. "Now to the lookout tower!"

The branches of the giant tree were easy to climb. From the platform, the cousins sat comfortably with their binoculars, looking out over the lake. A peninsula blocked their view of the water below Skull Cliff, but they could see over the ridge to where they'd stood just a few hours earlier. From this distance, the cliff truly resembled a skull. A waterfall poured from one of the "eyes," which made the skull appear to be weeping.

19

A police car was driving slowly through the picnic area. "Hey, guys, see where those cops are?" Claire said.

"Then, look over in the bushes, way off to the right."

Jeff and David stared through their lenses. After a moment, Jeff said, "Something's moving. Looks like a brown bear. Or maybe a grizzly?"

"Grizz," said David with confidence. "Definitely."

"But the cops are too far away to see it," Claire said. "It's just plain spooky. I mean, about Willie Stamper. One minute we were talking to him, the next he was gone." She swallowed, staring across the water.

Jeff and David were quiet. Yes, it was Grizzly Paw Wilderness. But a bear near those campsites could mean danger.

21

# 4
# Ransom Note

*T*he cousins canoed home from Lost Island in time to gather their camping gear. Their backpacks were stuffed with a change of clothes, their walkie-talkies, mess kits, sunscreen, flashlights, and dog food. Soon they saw Uncle Wyatt driving up the dirt road. As usual, he wore his cowboy hat.

"Ariel will meet us at the campground," he told them while helping the cousins load the jeep. Uncle Wyatt and Aunt Lilly were Claire's parents. They owned the Western Café in town.

Jeff, David, and Claire rode in the backseat, squished together in the middle, so the dogs could hang out the windows. As the town came into view, they were surprised to see a crowd and several police cars gathered by the café.

"Daddy, what's going on?" Claire asked.

"Volunteers are helping search for the boy," he answered, pulling into a parking space. "Your mom and I are making sandwiches and coffee for the officers. But right now, I need to pick up the produce for Camp Whispering Pines. Be right back."

While waiting for Uncle Wyatt, the brothers got out to look at one of the squad cars. They liked seeing the touch screen, GPS, and other gadgets on the dashboard.

"Hey, Jeff, David, come here." Claire was pulling them toward the outside table in front of the café. She whispered to them, "The ransom note is right there. By that officer's elbow. Can you see what it says?"

David leaned over for a look. The note looked like a list written on blue stationery. While he pulled out his sketch pad to copy down what he could, Jeff and Claire talked to the police captain, who was drinking coffee from a Styrofoam cup. He and the cousins had become friendly when they helped solve a couple of mysteries earlier in the summer.

"Sir, I called about the white pickup truck we saw, with a lady driving. We think it could have been Willie in the backseat."

"Anything unusual about the truck that would make it stand out?"

Jeff thought a moment. "Not really. Except it was going fast."

"Son, do you know how many white pickups are in this area? Every rancher and rodeo rider has a truck, and probably half of 'em are white. Plus, they all drive like their hair's on fire."

"Well, what about Willie's cell phone?" Claire asked. "Has anyone tried calling him?"

"We've called," the man replied. He took a sip of his coffee. "But it just rings and rings. Maybe the

23

kidnapper threw it away, or Willie's somewhere with no reception.

"Anyway," the captain continued, "it'll take a while to track his phone by satellite and the cell phone towers. Meanwhile, his parents are in Tibet visiting a monastery or some such thing, and it's going to take several days for them to get here. Listen, I've gotta get back to work. I'm afraid this is one case you kids won't be able to solve. Thanks for trying to help, though."

*B*ack in the jeep, David opened his sketchbook. Speaking in a low voice he said, "The note was torn around the edges and a lot of the words are missing. But I'm pretty sure I copied the words just like they were on the page." The cousins stared at the list:

This concerns
William Edward Stamper
transfer the funds kid
napping
must!!
he will die
make sure
VERY IMPORTANT!!
or else he will suffer

# don't forget the money
## senator
### will be in touch

"Looks like Willie's in real trouble," Claire said.

Uncle Wyatt turned down the dirt road to Camp Whispering Pines. He parked by the kitchen. The cousins helped him carry in several watermelons and baskets of strawberries.

While Uncle Wyatt spoke to the cook, the kids wandered into the dining hall, where there were long tables and benches. Three teenage boys were setting the tables with plates and bowls. They laughed as if sharing a good joke. Their T-shirts said junior counselor.

Even though the police captain said the cousins wouldn't be able to find Willie, they still wanted to try. They loved solving mysteries, which meant asking questions. Claire volunteered to go first.

"Excuse me," she said, approaching the teenagers who were still joking. "Do you know Willie Stamper?"

At the mention of the missing boy, the teens stopped laughing. "What about Willie Stamper?" one of them asked.

"Well, we heard about what happened and we were wondering—"

"Willie's a pain," said one boy. "A weirdo. He always wants to hang out with us instead of the kids his own age."

"Maybe he's lonely," Claire offered, remembering why Willie wanted to buy Yum-Yum. "I mean, I bet it's hard to make friends with a bunch of new kids every week, then say good-bye when they go home. I wouldn't like that."

"How old are you, anyway, little girl?" one of the teens asked her.

She crossed her arms and lifted her chin. "Nine," she said.

"Nine? Ha! You don't know what you're talking about."

"Oh, yes, I do," Claire insisted. "I'm an only child like Willie. If my parents dumped me at camp for the whole summer, I'd be plenty lonesome."

"Whatever."

Jeff cleared his throat and looked at the counselor who had not yet said anything. "Why do you guys think he's weird?" he asked.

"Here's the thing," the boy said. "Last night, Willie sneaked into the kitchen to use the phone and order his favorite pizza, pepperoni with anchovies. When it arrived, he paid for it and brought it to the JC lounge to share with us. He sat on our couch with those stinking anchovies and wanted to talk. He's twelve. We're seventeen. We're stuck with little

kids all day long, so at night we don't wanna hang
out with a—"

"Then what do you think happened to Willie?"
Jeff interrupted.

The young counselors fell silent. They gave one
another nervous looks. Then, turning away from the
cousins, they continued setting the tables for dinner.
"Beat it," one of them said, pointing to the screen
door. "We've got work to do here."

# 5
# Camping

*T*en minutes later, Uncle Wyatt drove farther up the hill toward Skull Cliff. In the backseat, the cousins discussed what had just happened in the dining hall.

"Those JCs don't like Willie Stamper, that's for sure."

"They acted suspicious, like they're hiding something."

"And they're mean."

The road was bumpy. David's pencil bounced as he sketched a map of the lake. It showed Camp Whispering Pines and Skull Cliff, but no trail connecting the two.

"How come you're not drawing this road we're on?" Claire asked.

Keeping his eye on his artwork, he replied, "It's more mysterious this way."

*A*riel's tent was bright blue with a green rain tarp over the top. Her butane stove sat on the picnic table, which she had decorated with some pinecones. She was frying ham and potatoes when the cousins appeared on the trail with their dogs trotting out in front. Their shadows were long. It was an hour before sunset.

"Hi, everyone!" she called, waving the spatula. Her brown hair was a mess of curls, held back by a bandana. Her eyes were green and friendly. "I'm so glad to see you kids. Dinner is in fifteen minutes, plenty of time to set up your tent. Pitch it over there by mine, far from the eating area. Hello, Mr. Posey!"

Uncle Wyatt lifted his cowboy hat to say hello, then walked back down the path to finish unloading the jeep. It was a rough, narrow road to this campsite from Skull Cliff. Ariel had chosen a spot in a grove of aspen and pine, sheltered from the wind. Her hybrid was parked under a tree with her special three-day pass on the dashboard. Just a few cars were permitted in the campground each night—no trailers or RVs with noisy generators. Because only tents were allowed, it was peaceful.

Uncle Wyatt tuned his walkie-talkie channel to Ariel's and the cousins'. It had a two-mile radius, so they would be able to contact one another if needed. "Have fun and be safe," he said, hugging Claire good-bye.

After Uncle Wyatt left, the cousins told Ariel about the bear they'd seen from their lookout tower. Besides their friend Mr. Wellback, she was the only one they had confided in about their fort on Lost Island. They also told her about Willie Stamper.

29

"Oh, that poor kid," said Ariel. "Maybe there'll be some good news tomorrow.

"Now, about that bear, we are in Grizzly Paw Wilderness and have to be extra careful. That's why I brought up just one day's worth of food, so that we finish most of it by tonight. We'll eat only here at the table, and if we spill on our clothes, they go in the bear bag. That also means insect repellent and candy, and, Claire, your cherry-lip balm. Dog food, too. Our tents are a safe distance from the picnic table—at least two hundred feet away—and I haven't seen any droppings or fresh claw marks on trees. But that doesn't mean a bear won't come in the night to snoop around."

The cousins adored Ariel. She wasn't afraid of being in the woods, and she knew how to take charge. After dinner, they filled a waterproof bag with their food and treats. Ariel even packed their sunscreen, because bears are attracted to strong smells.

"Boys, did you bring your parachute cord from last time? The one that's about fifty feet?"

"Got it!" Jeff dug through his pack.

"Can you still tie a good clove hitch?" she asked David. "You bet."

"Okay, Claire, how about you make a weight with this." Ariel pulled the bandana from her hair. "Fill it with dirt, then secure it to one end of Jeff's rope, like you did last time. Here we go."

Together they found a tree away from their campsite. Jeff threw the weighted cord over a tall branch. At the other end was the bear bag. They pulled until the bottom of the bag was twelve feet off the ground. They made sure it was eight feet away from the trunk. This was so that a bear couldn't climb up and reach out its paw to grab it. David tied the free end of the cord to another tree.

"Well done!" Ariel looked up at the swinging sack and noted the sky was pink from the setting sun. "Now if a bear comes sniffing, our campsite is clean and it'll go away. Okay, kiddos, it'll be dark soon. What do you want to do?"

They liked the way Ariel called them kiddos. And they especially liked how she would tell them stories. Scary stories.

"Could you tell us about Skull Cliff again?" Jeff asked. "The legend?"

"Oooh, you mean what happens when it's a full moon? And the mysterious moaning? That one?"

The cousins looked at one another, then nodded. "Yeah, that one!" they answered, already feeling a delicious shiver.

# 6

# The Legend

In the waning sunlight, the foursome washed their dishes in hot water that had been heating on the stove. Then the cousins gathered wood from the ground, thin enough to break with their hands.

Meanwhile, Ariel made a fire pan from an aluminum tray, which was perched on some rocks so that heat from the flames wouldn't damage the soil. Since Claire was the youngest, she got to strike the match against a stone. She lit the kindling of twigs and dried pine needles, and soon a warm campfire flickered before them.

"Well ... well ... well," Ariel began. She sat cross-legged on the ground, wearing jeans and a down vest over her shirt. Her curly hair was loose about her shoulders. "A long time ago," she said, "when this was the Wild West, mountain men and fur trappers roamed these parts. They wrestled grizzlies and ate fried beaver tail for dinner. They hunted buffalo. Most of them made friends with the Indians. Well, one summer night when a full moon lit the sky, some of these trappers saw diamonds sparkling on a ledge of Skull Cliff, in what looked like one of the eyes. They had heard about this amazing treasure and there it was, hidden in the rocks of the canyon wall. They couldn't believe their good fortune."

Claire zipped up her sweatshirt. It was now dark and the mountain air was cold. Jeff and David pulled on their hoodies. The dogs curled up at their feet, also listening to Ariel's story.

"The men," she continued, "decided to get those diamonds. They would be rich and could buy a mansion in San Francisco. No more sleeping out in the rain. Anyway, when they tried to scale the cliff—"

Ariel stopped. Rascal and Yum-Yum were growling. The two little dogs stared into the shadows. Even old Tessie, who was hard of hearing, growled low in her throat. The fur on her neck stood up straight.

"What is it, girl?" Jeff asked, holding on to her collar.

A stink of dead fish came on the breeze. "Smells like a bear," whispered Ariel. Her eyes scanned the dark forest.

Crack! Something moved in the brush. Now Tessie gave a ferocious woof-woof-woof. Rascal and Yum-Yum snarled and strained at their leashes.

Ariel listened, waiting. Claire started to whisper, but the brothers said, "Shh." They shone their flashlights around, but they saw nothing unusual. Eventually, the dogs quieted. Through the trees came the bright orb of the rising moon. It cast feathery shadows across the campsite. Their fire had died down to embers.

"Let's pour some water on this," said Ariel, "then turn in. We have two more nights here. Plenty of time for stories. And tomorrow, a special guest is joining us for dinner."

35

*C*laire lay snug in her sleeping bag, cuddling Yum-Yum. Drowsy, she thought about Willie Stamper and hoped he was all right. She was drifting to sleep when a crunching sound startled her. Her eyes flew open. There it was again: crunch ... crunch. Whatever it was, it sounded close. But why weren't the dogs growling? She leaned on her elbow.

Moonlight against their tent cast Jeff and David in silhouette. She could see their jaws moving.

"Are you guys eating something?" she said.

"Chocolate-covered almonds," David said. "Want some?"

Claire was stunned. "Here? After Ariel made us put everything in the bear bag? Even my lip balm!"

The brothers were quiet.

"These were in my pocket," David said. "I forgot."

"I can't believe you guys. Ariel won't take us camping anymore if we don't mind her."

"Claire, if you wanna get mad at someone, get mad at Jeff. He left his candy outside on the picnic table. It's there now."

"On the table? Where a bear can find it, then come after us?"

"I was planning to share at the campfire," Jeff explained, "so that everything would be gone by the time we went to bed. But the dogs made me forget."

36

"Jeff," said Claire. "You're the oldest. You're supposed to set a good example."

"I know. It was dumb. I'm sorry. I'll go get it."

"But we don't want food in here!" Claire was frustrated with her cousins. "Remember what happened to Mr. Wellback when he was a boy? The grizzly smelled the ham sandwiches in his tent and—"

Rascal and old Tessie were growling again. Yum-Yum crawled out of Claire's sleeping bag, also growling.

The cousins listened. Something was outside and it was moving toward them.

# 7
## Visitor in the Night

*C*laire reached for her walkie-talkie. Her hands were shaking.

"Ariel," she whispered. "Something's out there. Please answer. Over."

Jeff and David gobbled the remaining chocolates as fast as they could. It wasn't the best solution, but at the moment it was the only one they thought of. Then they sealed the wrapper in a zip-lock bag.

"Stay where you are," came Ariel's voice from the speaker. "I hear it, too. It'll probably go away in a minute. Over."

Jeff unzipped their tent enough to poke his flashlight through the opening. He aimed it about, searching the trees.

"What if it's the kidnapper?" David asked.

Jeff hesitated before saying, "Who would want to kidnap us?" He stopped moving the flashlight and held it steady. "Hey, guys, look," he  said. Claire and David crowded next to him to see outside. His light reflected a pair of eyes low in the brush. The eyes blinked, then there was another pair, then several shiny eyes stared out.

"This is scaring me," said Claire.

"Me, too," said David.

Jeff flicked off his light. He thought a moment. "I think it's the bear. And maybe her cubs."

The cousins didn't know what to do. Through the wall of their tent they could see a shadow moving across their moonlit campsite. It was round and low to the ground. Jeff looked outside again. This time, he laughed. "Guys, it's just a raccoon with three babies."

David gave a loud sigh of relief.

At this good news, Claire notified Ariel. "Everything's okay. Over." Even though their tents were just a few feet apart, Claire didn't want to holler into the night. Besides, she liked using the walkie-talkies.

"Good night, then. See you kiddos for breakfast. Over."

The next morning at sunrise, the cousins crawled out of their tent. Only David was still wearing the clothes he had slept in. The ground was wet from a light rainfall, and they could see their breath in the damp air. They walked their dogs, picking up after them with plastic bags.

*Leave only footprints,* the boys' father had taught them. *This keeps the wilderness clean for everyone to enjoy.*

39

Ariel was already at the camp stove heating water for hot chocolate. She had started a small campfire and taken the bear bag down from the tree. On the table were a jug of maple syrup, pancake mix, and a carton of orange juice. Three bowls were filled with dog kibble.

"Morning!" she called. "Boys, how 'bout you stir up the batter and set the table? Claire, you can help me here. Looks like our visitor inspected camp last night but left without causing trouble. Good thing we hoisted all our smellables high off the ground."

Jeff and David glanced at their cousin, hoping she wouldn't tell what really happened. But Claire smiled at them with her mouth shut to show she was keeping this matter to herself. *Good ol' Claire*, the brothers thought.

They searched for Jeff's candy but, of course, it was gone. And there was no sign of its wrapper, either. But they did find something else. David pointed to tracks in the soggy ground. They were much bigger than a raccoon's but smooshed together from the rain, so they couldn't make out the toes or claws.

"There really was a bear by our tent!" David cried.

The campground had a pleasant aroma of wood smoke and frying bacon. Ariel gave them each a mug of steaming chocolate when they sat down to breakfast.

"So," she said, "any plans for today?"

40

Claire dribbled syrup on her pancakes in neat little circles. "I keep thinking about Willie Stamper. Let's take the shuttle to town and see if they caught the kidnapper."

"Or," said David, kicking his older brother under the table, "maybe we could do something interesting for a change, like track the bear we saw from the lookout tower."

"We'll be sooo careful," Jeff said, kicking his brother so he would nod in agreement. "You girls go to town and we'll meet you back here for dinner."

Ariel bit her lip to keep from laughing. "So you two want to find that bear, do you? By yourselves?"

The brothers nodded. "Sure. We'll take our walkie- talkies."

"And we'll whistle on the trail, so we don't come upon it by surprise." David wanted Ariel to know that he knew the rules for being safe in bear country.

"Gentlemen," said Ariel, making a quick decision. "Here's what we're going to do. After cleaning up camp, we'll all go to town for groceries, then we'll cool off in the lake."

"But why?"

Ariel reached into her pocket and held up an empty bag of chocolates. "Does this look familiar to anyone?" At this, the boys looked away, ashamed. "All right, then," she said, "you kiddos

41

can explore on your own later. But this morning, the four of us are sticking together."

# 8

# A Surprise Suspect

*T*he bus stopped at the marina, where the cousins found a shady tree for their dogs. They gave them water from their canteens, then went into the bait shop, which also sold groceries. Its wooden floors creaked as they wandered the aisles for dinner ideas. Ariel had told them they could plan any meal they wanted as long as the leftovers would fit into the bear bag at night.

At the checkout counter, they overheard the cashier talking to another customer. "Well," she said, "the police have almost pinpointed the boy's cell phone. It's somewhere up near Table Rock. At this very moment, rangers are on their way, but their search will probably take all day."

"Table Rock?" Claire couldn't help herself.

"That's the weird thing," the cashier said to the group now gathered at her register. "It's been twenty-four hours, and the kidnapper hasn't called about the ransom."

In a low voice, with everyone leaning close to hear her, the cashier added, "Someone said his daddy's a senator from the Green City resort area and the boy's walking around with a pocketful of fifty-dollar bills. He could've hopped on a train for all we know."

The cousins hurried out of the store whispering to one another.

"What if Willie wrote his own ransom note?"

"Then why would those junior counselors act suspicious?"

"Maybe they helped Willie run away."

Jeff noticed Ariel on the beach. "Come on, guys. Ariel's waiting for us. Let's put this stuff in her cooler."

After a picnic of cheese sandwiches and grapes, the cousins waded into the cold lake. In the roped-off area, they swam out to a floating raft and pulled themselves up the slimy ladder. Two teenage girls were there, sunbathing. They were discussing rattlesnakes, which immediately interested the brothers.

"Have you ever seen one up close?" David asked. "Last summer, one came up on our porch."

"Big deal," said the younger girl. "Our brother got bitten yesterday and almost died. So there."

David felt like pushing this sassy girl off the raft but knew it wouldn't be nice. Jeff asked, "Where was the snake?"

"Skull Cliff," she answered. "Our mom drove him to the hospital."

Claire caught her breath. "Was she driving a white pickup?"

44

"Yeah. Mom was so freaked, she forgot us, so we had to take the stupid shuttle back to the lodge."

From where the cousins lay on the raft, they could see across the lake to Skull Cliff. Without saying so, they all now knew Willie Stamper had not been in that truck.

*B*ack at their campsite, the cousins helped Ariel hoist their groceries into the tree. She said they could go off on their own, as long as they stayed nearby. So they hiked to the ledge, where they could see the stony profile of Skull Cliff. Just beyond was Table Rock, another popular tourist spot. With their binoculars they searched the trails and bluff. Two jeeps from the forest service were there with flashing lights.

"Look!" cried David. "They have a man in handcuffs. He's got white hair and a white beard."

"They must have tracked him with Willie's cell phone signal," Jeff said.

"But I don't see Willie," said Claire. "Where's Willie?" Jeff's binoculars were large, nearly covering his face.

"Oh, no," he said. "That's Mr. Wellback they're arresting!"

"Our friend, Mr. Wellback? Dad's old hiking buddy?" The cousins let their binoculars hang from their necks.

They couldn't believe it.

Claire's voice was quiet. "So why would Mr. Wellback have Willie's cell phone?"

# 9
# New Clues

The cousins hurried back to the campground. They told Ariel about Mr. Wellback.

"Oh, no!" she said. "That can't be. He's supposed to be our guest tonight. His tent and sleeping bag are in my car. I was going to surprise you since he's an old friend of all of our families."

Ariel paused and gave them a serious look. "It's two o'clock. Can I trust you kiddos to stay safe for the rest of the afternoon?"

"Of course," Claire answered.

"Then I'm going to the police station. This must be a terrible mistake. Gus Penny would never do anything dishonorable." Gus Penny was the elderly man's real name. But the cousins called him Mr. Wellback, because he always began his stories by saying, "Well, back in the olden days ... "

Ariel filled her canteen from the water spigot. "Okay," she said. "I'll meet you three, and your dogs, back here before sunset."

Though Claire was only nine, she took charge of her older cousins. She rummaged through her daypack and pulled out three plastic grocery bags. "First we should do a good deed."

"What!"

"Yep." Claire handed each boy a bag. "There's a ton of trash from those city kids. All sorts of stuff in the bushes. If we pick it up, we're helping keep the wilderness clean, like your dad said. Ready? It won't take long."

The boys wanted to honor their father, but today they felt like goofing off. They trudged after their cousin. They jumped on soda cans to crush them flat. They picked up orange peels, Popsicle sticks, and paper. They hurled dirt clods at each other's feet. They threw sticks for the dogs to fetch.

At last, Claire ordered everyone to rest and whistled for the dogs. Yum-Yum and Rascal curled up in the shade of a little pine tree. Then, after some rustling in the brush, Tessie appeared, carrying something small and white in her mouth. She was old but still liked to retrieve things.

"Drop it," the boys instructed. What fell to their feet looked like a deck of cards, gooey from being in Tessie's mouth.

David picked it up. "What's an iPod doing here?" He inspected it. "No name anywhere. It's missing its cord and ear-buds. Should we leave it, in case the owner comes looking?"

"No way," said Jeff. "They'd never find it. And we don't know exactly where Tessie picked it up. We should turn it in to the next ranger we see. But first let's see what else we can find."

They followed Tessie's path through the sagebrush, careful to avoid poison ivy along the creek. The dogs led them to a dry streambed. The stones were brushed aside as if someone had tried to make a soft spot in the sand.

Charred twigs, gum wrappers, and some empty sardine tins were in a blackened pile with several books of burned matches.

"*P–U*," said David, picking up one of the tins. "Smells like that bear last night. Think his claws tore these things wide open?"

Jeff knelt in the dirt, looking for clues. "I wonder. Hey, look. Someone tried to start a fire here but didn't know how. Wasted a ton of matches. Speaking of bears, look at these giant paw prints. They're exactly like the ones we saw this morning by our tent."

David picked up the other sardine tins for his trash bag. "These things stink like anchovies."

Claire's mouth dropped open with surprise. "Anchovies!" she cried. "Remember what the JCs said about Willie's favorite pizza, pepperoni and anchovies? What if he's the one who was here last night eating these smelly things, not a bear? He probably keeps some in his backpack. Like how I carry granola bars in mine."

Now the cousins stared at the paw prints. After a moment, Jeff said, "Actually, these look human, don't you think? They're missing the claw marks, just like the ones by our tent."

"Yeah," David agreed, disappointed. "But there's no tread, like with sneakers or hiking boots. These look like —"

50

"—like flip-flops!" Jeff exclaimed. "Like what Willie was wearing. There's only one set of prints, so if he was here, he was alone. I bet Willie was watching our campfire last night."

"If he was alone, then maybe he wasn't kidnapped," Claire said. "It looks like all he did was walk by our tent and eat Jeff's candy. He could've yelled for help but didn't."

David shrugged. "I don't get it. If Willie wasn't kidnapped, why is there a ransom note with his name on it?"

The cousins looked at one another. There seemed to be more questions than ever.

Finally, Jeff said, "Maybe we should talk to those JCs again. I think they know something. And maybe there's a clue in Willie's cabin."

# 10
# A Tiny Chalet

*T*he cousins took their garbage to the picnic area, where there was a Dumpster. It was full, so they set their bags on top of it, hoping trash would be picked up soon so it wouldn't attract a bear. Then they walked down the road with their dogs to Camp Whispering Pines.

In the kitchen, they said hello to the cook, who knew them from their deliveries with Claire's father. He was friendly and eager to help them.

"Let's see," he said as he was stirring strawberries into a giant fruit salad. "The JCs are on the lake this afternoon with some campers—won't be back till suppertime. But you can see Willie's cabin across the yard, under that big oak tree. The police locked it for safekeeping."

With his wooden spoon, the cook pointed out the screen door to a tiny chalet with moose antlers hanging above the door. It was near the nurse's station. "The senator and Mrs. Stamper wanted Willie to be close to the infirmary in case he gets sick," he explained. "I just hope the searchers find him before he gets bronchitis—or worse. It gets cold in the mountains at night."

*T*he cousins peered in the window of Willie's cabin. A bed with mussed-up blankets was against one wall. The floor was littered with clothes and comic books. A teddy bear had been thrown in a corner.

"How come there's only one bed?" asked David.

"Poor Willie!" Claire cried. "In a cabin all by himself, for the whole summer. No wonder he wants a dog."

Jeff tapped on the window, pointing inside. "Guys, see that thing plugged into the wall?"

"You mean the charger?"

"Yeah," Jeff replied. "Looks like it's for an iPod."

"Wow!" David took the iPod from his pocket. "So this really could be Willie's! So he probably was by our campsite."

Claire cupped her hands to the window to see inside. "Hey, look at that crumpled-up paper."

"Yeah?"

"It's blue," she said. "So?"

"David, remember the ransom note you copied? It was on blue paper, right?"

"Right."

"Well, maybe Willie wrote his own ransom note," Claire again suggested.

Suddenly, David picked up Rascal and began hurrying toward the road. "Here comes the shuttle bus," he called over his shoulder. "If we wave to the driver, he'll stop and let us get on. We've gotta get back to Skull Cliff, quick. I just remembered something."

54

*T*he Dumpster in the picnic area hadn't been emptied yet. The cousins' three bags were still on top. David rushed over and dumped out the trash they had gathered earlier. He rifled through it with his foot.

"David!" Claire protested. "We worked hard to clean that up!"

"What are you doing?" Jeff asked his younger brother. "I thought this looked familiar!" David shouted. He waved a torn piece of blue stationery. Without a word, he took his sketch pad from his pack and flipped it open to the words he had copied yesterday at the command post. Like a puzzle piece, he wiggled the paper on either side of the note until it fit.

Though some of the words were smudged from the rain, the cousins could tell this was part of the ransom note. "Let's look for more pieces!" Claire cried.

Carefully, they searched the trash. Then they again walked through the brush, bending low to see under branches. Finally, Jeff found a boulder where wind had blown leaves and bits of cardboard. Pushing aside the debris, he uncovered another piece of blue stationery. This one was dry. He took it back to David's sketchbook and fit it on the page.

"There're still some missing corners," Jeff said, "but listen." He read aloud:

To the camp director:
This concerns William Edward Stamper. If he needs spending money, transfer the funds from our camp deposit to his account. Since he's a rowdy kid, napping every afternoon is a must!! He will die of embarrassment without clean socks and shirts, so make sure his laundry is done. He must use sunscreen. THIS IS VERY IMPORTANT!! or else he will suffer from blisters and burns. Don't forget the money is in our Whispering Pines account. Sincerely, Senator and Mrs. Stamper. We will be in touch soon.

"No way is this about ransom," Jeff declared. "It's just a note from his mom."

"She sure treats him like a baby," said Claire. "We never have to take naps. And David doesn't mind dirty socks."

"Not a bit," David agreed. "Hey, I wonder why the camp director tore this up."

"What if he never got it?" Jeff reasoned. "David, if Mom wrote like this, we'd rip it up before anyone could see it. Maybe Willie throws away all her letters."

"Okay. Since this isn't a ransom note, he wasn't kidnapped, right?"

"Right."

"Then where could he be?"

The cousins looked over at Skull Cliff and the blue lake. They felt sorry for the city boy alone in the woods without a sleeping bag or a tent.

Claire sighed. "Remember after Willie tried to buy Yum-Yum, he was showing off like he had something to prove?"

"Yeah," David said. "On his cell phone he pretended he was talking to his friend, but it was really his mom."

Jeff nodded slowly. "Guys, I think Willie's out here somewhere trying to prove he isn't a baby."

"I have a really bad feeling about all this," Claire said.

"Me, too," said David.

# 11
# Full Moon

*A*s the afternoon sun moved lower in the sky, the cousins kept searching the nearby trails and sagebrush. They were worried for Willie. Jeff called Ariel on his walkie-talkie.

"Ariel," he said, holding down the button on his handset. "Willie wasn't kidnapped. Tell the police captain that we found the other pieces of the note. It's from his mother. Over."

"You're kidding!" came Ariel's voice. "I'll tell 'im. You kiddos okay up there? Over."

"We're fine. Can we start the campfire? Over."

Crackling came from the speaker. "Go for it. I'll be there soon. Over."

*J*ust before sunset the last shuttle came up the hill from Cabin Creek. The cousins were cleaning the picnic table when Ariel and Mr. Wellback came through the brush. The white-haired man raised his hiking stick in greeting.

"They near threw me in the slammer," he said, setting his rucksack on the ground. "I was madder than a wet cat when that pollywog put the cuffs on me."

Pollywog was his name for the young rangers in green shirts.

"So why did they try to arrest you?" Jeff asked. "Did the cops find Willie's cell phone?"

Mr. Wellback lowered himself onto a large rock by the fire. He slapped a mosquito from his arm, ignoring the question.

Ariel answered for him. "The cell phone was in his rucksack."

"Really?"

"If you must know," he grumbled, "I found the blasted thing on my hike up here yesterday. I was planning on turning it in at the lodge. Excuse me for living, but I was enjoying some peace and quiet without TV last night. Didn't know the town was turned inside out about a missing kid."

"But people were calling Willie's number," said Claire. "Why didn't you answer his phone?"

Mr. Wellback scratched his beard. Then he looked over at Ariel, so she would explain.

She said, "Willie must have turned the ringer to vibrate before he lost his phone. Gus just thought he was hearing a rattler—you know, a snake—so

59

he kept walking and walking. Not until the rangers came—"

"Tadpoles!"

"The rangers just thought he was playing dumb," said Ariel. "They couldn't believe that in this day and age someone wouldn't know about  —"

"Anyhow," Mr. Wellback said, changing the subject. "I hope you scallywags are making your specialty again, beans and franks. Here, I brought you some graham crackers for dessert. I am roaring hungry. How can I help?"

David jumped up. "Stay where you are, sir!" He handed everyone a long twig that he had soaked in the stream. The wet sticks wouldn't burn over the flames while the hot dogs were roasting.

The cousins had forgotten to buy mustard and pickle relish, but they did have a large can of baked beans. Claire peeled off the label and opened the can so its lid was still partially attached. Now Jeff took pliers from his pack and carefully bent the lid backward until it formed a smooth handle. He wedged it among some rocks in the fire.

"Now that's camp cookin'," Mr. Wellback said. "Just like your dad and I used to do. Once we boiled up a tin of olives by mistake—the label had come off—but we were hungry enough to eat 'em all."

Jeff and David smiled. They loved hearing stories about their father. He and Mr. Wellback had gone backpacking in the wilderness every summer, before the boys were born.

As the campers ate dinner, small winged creatures began swooping into camp, close to the ground.

"Bats," David announced with his usual confidence.

"No, sonny," said Mr. Wellback. "They're swallows—eating bugs that have flown in with wet wings. It's from the low-pressure system."

"What's that?" asked Claire.

Jeff answered, "It means a storm is coming."

Under the light of the rising moon, Mr. Wellback pitched his tent while the cousins raised the bear bag. Ariel brought out a folding chair.

"For my cricky bones," he said, thanking her. "Now what story would you troublemakers like—"

"The legend!" they cried, warm in their sweatshirts and ready to be scared.

"The legend of Skull Cliff, huh? Well, back in the olden days, when I was a boy," he began in his deep voice, "the counselors at Camp Whispering Pines warned us to stay away from Skull Cliff during a full moon."

"Why?"

"To scare us. So we'd stay in our cabins and not wander into danger."

"What kind of danger?"

"The diamond kind," answered Mr. Wellback. "On nights with a full moon, you can see into one of the eyes of the skull. There's a rocky ledge there, impossible to get to. But in the moonlight, if you look past the little waterfall coming from the eye socket, you can see the jewels sparkling and winking from inside the skull, daring you to come take them."

"Who put the diamonds there in the first place?" Claire wanted to know.

The old man leaned toward the fire and stirred the coals with his stick. The embers hissed, casting his face in an orange glow.

He looked every child in the eye, then said, "One snowy winter long ago, a prospector was returning to Cabin Creek with his newfound fortune. He planned to surprise his beloved wife, but he was delayed by a blizzard. When he finally arrived, he learned that she had died days earlier on her way to meet his stagecoach. The horse she was riding had fallen through the ice."

Mr. Wellback continued, "Her husband was so heartbroken, he hid his treasure, then left town as poor as the day he had married—when he was penniless but happily in love. The legend says that anyone who has searched for the diamonds during a full moon has gone missing. If you hear a loud moaning coming from the cliff, it's the lovelorn cry of the dead wife."

David swallowed hard. "You mean a ... ghost?"

"According to legend, yes," Mr. Wellback answered. "No one has been able to claim the treasure because the ghost of the bride protects it. She wants only her true love to retrieve the jewels."

The cousins were quiet. Wind was beginning to rustle the trees and chill the air. A wisp of clouds now dimmed the moonlight.

"Have any kids ever ... gone missing?" Claire asked in a trembly voice.

Mr. Wellback stood up, leaning on his hiking stick. "I think it's time we all turn in," he said.

# 12
# A Terrifying Noise

Snug in their tent with their dogs, the cousins whispered. "Here's my theory," said Jeff. "Maybe Willie heard about the legend, so he took off on his own to find the diamonds."

"I've been wondering about that, too," said Claire. She held Yum-Yum close. "But if Willie's out here roaming around, he's in danger from bears. Plus his daypack was too small for a blanket or extra food. I bet he's cold and starving."

"Then why hasn't he come back here for help?"

"Maybe he got lost," Claire suggested. "Or hurt. We should look for him right now!"

A loud snap startled them. But it was just the sides of their tent billowing out from the wind. "The storm's coming fast," Jeff reminded her.

Claire was already putting her sweatshirt back on. "But, Jeff, can't we take a quick look? If Willie figured out how to start a fire, we might see his smoke. I can radio Daddy, then he can call the police."

"Guys?" It was David. "What about the ghost? It's a full moon tonight."

Jeff grabbed his flashlight. "Mr. Wellback said it's just a legend, remember? Come on, let's hurry." He unzipped the tent as quietly as possible.

Wind shook the sagebrush and swirled dust in the air as the cousins headed out into the moonlight with their dogs. Shadows from the trees swayed over them. They looked in every direction for smoke or a glowing fire, but there was no sign of Willie. Even their campground was dark. The other families had doused their coals to keep sparks from flying. No one wanted a forest fire.

After some minutes on the trail, they came to an overhang with the lake far below. They leashed their dogs to a tree for safety. Then they crept to the edge, where they could see Skull Cliff, just around the bend. They stared at the moonlit rock.

"Wow!" Jeff said. "It sure looks like a skull from here. I wish we remembered the binoculars. I can't see any diamonds."

"Me, neither." David glanced up at the full moon. "Maybe the ghost is hiding them. Let's get outta here!"

"Wait, look!" said Claire. "Something sparkly is behind the waterfall. See? There it is!"

But just then, a strong gust of wind hit them and the moon vanished behind clouds. Now in total darkness, they stood on the rim of the cliff. They grabbed one another's sleeves and backed up toward the trail.

A moan startled them. It was loud and deep, like a foghorn. It lasted several seconds, then stopped. Then it started again.

The cousins clung to one another, feeling shivery and scared. They held their breaths. As they listened, the moaning grew louder.

"What ... is ... that?"

"I knew there was a ghost!" David cried above the storm. "She's calling for her husband!"

Jeff flicked on his flashlight. They ran in its bouncing light through the darkness until they found their dogs and untied their leashes from the tree. Raindrops began prickling their hands and faces. The noise rose in the wind like a fearsome howl.

Just as it started pouring, the cousins reached their tent. But Yum-Yum and Rascal wouldn't go in. They ran in circles, whining.

Suddenly, Claire cried, "Where's Tessie? She was right behind us!"

The children stared into the black night. They called her name, but the storm drowned out their voices. When the old Lab didn't appear, they grew frantic.

"What if she's near the cliff? It's dark and she'll fall!" David worried.

Jeff said, "I'm going after her. You guys stay here with your flashlights so I can see you." Then the older boy ran back to the trail. His light was fuzzy in the rain as he swung it back and forth. "Tessie!" came his muffled cry.

Claire and David waited in the cold wind, hanging tight to the little dogs. They shone their lights against the tent to make it glow. At last they saw the pale shape of Tessie loping toward them, followed by Jeff.

"That was close!" he cried. "She was by a tree digging for something, but her leash got caught on a branch. I should never have let go of her."

Safe inside, the cousins hurried to zip the door closed. They removed their wet sweatshirts while the dogs shook out the water from their fur. Then Tessie retreated to her blanket, carrying something in her mouth.

"What's she got this time? Drop it, girl." Jeff shone his light on her.

Tessie obeyed. A pouch made of brown canvas rolled out of her mouth. David picked it up.

"Hey, Dad used to have one of these," he said. "For rock climbing. Remember, Jeff?"

"Yeah. It holds chalk dust, for your fingers. So you can grip on to the side of a cliff. It went on his belt. Wonder where this came from."

Claire noticed an emblem: "Green City Climbing Wall, Junior Team. Uh-oh." She looked at her cousins. "Isn't Willie from Green City? Do you think this is his?"

While the noise outside continued, the cousins examined the bag. Jeff nodded. "Maybe Willie didn't know that climbing walls in a gym are safer than scaling rocks in the wilderness," he said. "Gyms don't have loose stones than can hit you in the head."

"I bet he's out here somewhere," said Claire. "We keep finding signs of him—like maybe his iPod and footprints and maybe those sardine tins. And remember in our lookout tower when we thought we saw a bear? Well, what if it was Willie? He has brown hair and his shirt is brown."

The beating of wind against their tent made it hard for them to hear one another. Rain spit against the nylon walls. They burrowed into their sleeping bags to get warm, their dogs nestled beside them.

The storm continued through the night.

Poor Willie, the cousins thought, as they lay wide awake.

# 13
## "Danger!"

*A*n hour before sunrise, the rain stopped. A breeze swept away the clouds, revealing a bright moon setting in the western sky. The air was cool and the ground puddled with mud.

The cousins crept out of their tent and quietly hurried to the rim with their dogs. In the moonlight, Skull Cliff looked like a pale face.

"It's so close. Let's get over there and check it out," Jeff whispered.

They hiked along a wooded trail and soon came to the parking lot. At that early hour, it was empty. Pinecones that had fallen in the storm dotted the picnic area.

The kids tied up their dogs. Around the bend was a large flat rock with warning signs:

**DANGER! KEEP OFF!** This was the bald top of Skull Cliff. Its surface was smooth and slippery. They could hear the waterfall as it splashed from the eye of the skull.

"Do you think Willie climbed out there?" asked Claire. "Then lowered himself down?"

"I hope not," Jeff said. "But that chalk bag makes me think he wanted to."

70

the dirt, but saw nothing. They listened. There it was again—kc*h* ... *kch* ... *kch*. Now they noticed the rope wiggle, ever so slightly.

"Willie!" they yelled, once again crawling to the rim. "Are you there?" They tugged the line to get his attention.

Finally, they saw a hand reaching out through the waterfall.

"Willie, stay there! We're not going to leave you. Help's coming!" They backed away from the edge, to where it was safe.

Claire called her dad on her walkie-talkie, then she called Ariel.

Moments later, Ariel appeared on the trail with Mr. Wellback. They were both out of breath.

"Great thunder!" declared the old man. "It's lucky that whippersnapper's not dead."

Jeff and David were too worked up to stand still. Claire was pacing. To her cousins, she whispered, "Did you see what I saw?"

The brothers nodded. "Yeah."

Willie's hand was missing two fingers.

## 14

# More Questions

*R*escue trucks with flashing red lights parked at Skull Cliff. A crowd of tourists gathered in the picnic area. They were held back by police officers directing traffic.

The cousins watched as a stretcher was pulled up and over the rim. Rangers had wrapped Willie in a blanket and strapped him in securely. Only his face showed. It was puffy and red from sunburn. His eyes were so swollen, he couldn't see the three children who had found him.

"Can we visit him in the hospital?" Claire asked the paramedics.

"Suit yourself," answered one. "Make sure it's all right with your folks first. This kid is eaten raw by mosquitoes and poison ivy."

"Is he going to die?" asked David.

"Well," came the reply, "let's just say he's in bad shape."

"What about his hand?" Jeff asked. "Beats me. The kid's not talking."

The ambulance took off in a spray of dirt. Its siren wailed all the way down the twisty road into town.

"*E*at some breakfast first," Ariel told the cousins. She set a carton of milk on the table and ladled hot oatmeal into three bowls. "Then you can visit Willie in the hospital. Gus and I'll stay here in camp with the dogs."

Mr. Wellback was revved up on his third cup of coffee. "Why in the hee-haw are you going to bother that boy? He doesn't need a lecture from you scallywags."

"We just want to ask him a few questions," Claire insisted.

"Such as?"

"Like, how he chopped off his fingers," David said. Instead of eating his oatmeal, David was drawing. First was Skull Cliff with a winking eye. Then he sketched Willie as a rock climber with a hand dripping in blood.

"And if Willie found any diamonds," Jeff said.

"Also," said Claire, "we wonder about the legend, why people go missing if they look for those jewels. And during the storm last night, what about that spooky howl—"

Mr. Wellback thumped his cup on the picnic table, sloshing out some coffee. "Do you people have a dictionary here?"

Jeff answered, "We're camping, sir."

"That we are, sonny. How 'bout you bring me my rucksack hanging from that branch over there. Thank you." Mr. Wellback dug into a pouch, then held up a paperback book.

"Webster's Dictionary," he said. "Every thinking person should have one of these. Missy, look up the word legend." He handed it to Claire.

She thumbed through the ragged pages. "A story," she read, "or a myth, often based on a kernel of truth. Fiction. What's fiction?"

"It means 'pretend,'" he answered. "Not real. Now what do you rascals think about the legend of Skull Cliff?"

Claire crossed her arms. "It was all a story? What a rip-off."

Jeff agreed. "Mountain men would've gotten those diamonds. Or someone would have. Maybe the moon shining on the water makes those sparkles—"

"Definitely," David declared, suddenly sure of himself. "That's exactly what I thought. But how come we didn't hear that howling last summer when we camped up here?"

76

Mr. Wellback raised his bushy white eyebrows. "Remember anything different from last year?"

The cousins looked at one another. Then all at once, they exclaimed, "No storm!"

The old man nodded. "Go on," he said. "I can tell you've got on your thinking caps."

Claire pointed to the sky. "I bet it was the wind last night, or something like that."

"Yes!" cried Jeff. "Wind through those canyon walls. I knew it!"

"Me, too," David said.

# 15
# New Friends

At the hospital, the cousins found Willie's room on the third floor. When they heard voices from behind his privacy curtain, they waited in the hall.

"Dude, we're really sorry," a young man was saying. "We were only joking."

"Yeah," said another, "we dare campers all the time, but we didn't think you'd actually go looking."

"I used to think you guys were cool," said Willie, "and that maybe we could be friends, but really you were just making fun of me. You're mean. You promised you'd tell me the rest of the legend—"

"Some other time, dude. We gotta go." At that, three teenage boys hurried from the room to the elevator.

Jeff whispered, "The JCs! So that's why they acted guilty. They're the ones who started this whole mess, daring Willie to find the diamonds. At least when Mr. Wellback was a kid, his counselors used the legend to keep campers away from danger."

Willie was hooked up to a machine with tubes feeding liquid into his arm. Both hands were wrapped in gauze His eyes were still swollen, but he could see his visitors. His sunburned lips moved as if he were trying to smile. "Hey."

"Hi, Willie," the three said, introducing themselves. "Here's your iPod. Our dog Tessie found it."

"Wow, thanks. I thought it was lost for good."

"How you doin'?" they asked.

He shrugged. "Boy, was I glad to hear you guys calling my name. That ledge inside the cliff was so small I was getting ready to jump into the lake after sitting for so long. But that howling! It freaked me out so bad, I couldn't move. Plus it was so cold last night, I changed my mind about swimming."

"We're glad you didn't jump," said Jeff. "Will your parents ground you?"

Again Willie tried to smile. "Yeah. But it was worth it. They always say I'll never do anything on my own. Well, they're wrong."

Claire came alongside Willie's bed and patted his shoulder. "You were brave all right," she said, "but it's really dumb to wander around by yourself. You could've gotten eaten by a bear."

Willie looked away. "I'm sorry for all the trouble I caused."

David took out his sketch pad. First he showed Willie the note he had copied. "This is why everyone thought you'd been kidnapped."

"Oh," Willie groaned. "My mom's letters are so embarrassing. I didn't want the counselors to make me take a nap, so I ripped up that one while we were on the hike. Hey, what's that picture?"

79

David showed him his drawing of Willie rock climbing. "Awesome," said the boy. "Can I keep it?"

"It's for you."

"But what's with the dripping blood?" asked Willie. His voice was beginning to sound lively.

"From your chopped-off fingers," David answered. "Were the rocks that sharp?"

"Huh?" Willie furrowed his brow. "Oh! You mean this?" He held up one of his covered hands. "I had an accident when I was ten. I was climbing on the roof and fell through a skylight. When I grabbed on to an edge, the glass cut right through two fingers. We were way out at a country inn and couldn't get to the hospital in time for the doctors to sew 'em back on. My parents flipped out. They wanted me to become a piano player or a surgeon, but now I'm just"—Willie paused —"well, anyway, they worry too much."

Claire remembered that first day, how Willie kept his hands in his pockets. And how he turned away to answer his cell phone. "So why are you bandaged up now?" she asked.

"The doctors want me to stop scratching my eyes. I didn't know about poison ivy and I got it pretty much everywhere. Hey, you guys want to visit my place sometime? We have a house on the beach for vacations. Oh, I almost forgot. Look in my backpack, there by the window. I found something yesterday. It was hidden behind the waterfall."

80

# 16
# Beauty

Jeff held an old leather pouch in his hands. It was empty and partly rotted.

"Wow!" the cousins exclaimed. "Was there anything else?"

"Just dirt and pebbles," Willie replied. "I thought for sure there would be some kind of treasure. The JCs told me they would explain the whole legend next week, when the new campers show up. They dared me to climb down the cliff, said I'd never be able to figure it out for myself. Do you guys know the story?"

Claire raised her hand so she could start first, as if she were in school. "Well, back in the olden days"—she laughed because this was how Mr. Wellback began his stories—"back long ago during winter, a rich man was returning to Cabin Creek to give his bride a fabulous gift. She was very beautiful and was expecting a baby."

"But there was a terrible blizzard," David continued, "that went on for weeks. It was way below zero. Icicles hanging from the roof of the general store were three feet long."

The cousins took turns telling Willie about the tragedy. They added colorful details as they went along, to make the story more interesting.

"So how did this bag get up there behind the waterfall?" Willie asked.

Claire looked out the window at the lake. "The brokenhearted husband threw it there, to hide his treasure. Since his beloved wife had died, he didn't want anyone else to have the diamonds that he planned to give her on their anniversary."

"But I have a question," David said. "Since it's only a legend, why did Willie actually find a bag?"

"I know!" cried Claire. "Remember what the dictionary said? That sometimes legends are based on real things?"

Now Jeff was wondering. "So," he said, "since the bag is real, why weren't there any diamonds? Is that part of the story made up?"

Willie eased himself onto his elbow. "Guys, I think I know."

The cousins waited for him to explain.

"Okay," Willie began. "When I let myself down on the rope, it took forever, but finally my toes touched the eye of Skull Cliff. Real quick, I ducked onto the ledge and crouched down. But there were all these wet little stones that made it slippery. The JCs hadn't said anything about diamonds, and besides, these weren't shiny or anything. I brushed them out with my hand."

82

"Brushed them out?" asked Jeff. "You mean, down into the lake?"

Willie nodded. "Down into the lake."

The four children regarded one another.

"Maybe they were just stones," Claire offered.

"I bet they were the diamonds!" David said with certainty. "All brown and dirty from being up there so long."

Now Willie sat up straight. He seemed to be feeling better by the minute. "Hey, when the doctors say I can leave here, let's go look in the lake. We might find something really cool."

A cart rattling with medicine rolled into the room. A nurse glared at the cousins. "What on earth are you kids doing up here?"

"They're my friends," Willie said.

"Doesn't matter. It's way past visiting hours. Now scram, the three of you."

*T*he shuttle stopped by the picnic area at Skull Cliff. When the cousins got out, they noticed a group of campers with easels and paintbrushes, facing the lake. A woman was instructing them.

Claire caught her breath. "Look," she whispered to the brothers. "It's that lady from the other day. Remember, she wore sunglasses and acted suspicious, like a kidnapper?"

"Yeah," said Jeff. "She was on her cell phone. Said she was going to teach spoiled rich kids a lesson they wouldn't forget."

The cousins sat on a nearby boulder so they could listen.

"Clouds can have the most beautiful shades of gray," the woman was saying. "Look around you. Watch how the lake reflects colors from the sky."

After some minutes, the cousins smiled at one another.

Now they understood what the woman had meant. She was teaching these city kids about the beauty of nature. It was an important lesson.

They hiked to their campground. As they came through the sagebrush, they saw their dogs asleep under the picnic table. Mr. Wellback and Ariel were playing a game of Scrabble.

Suddenly, Jeff had an idea.

"Guys, when Willie gets out of the hospital, let's ask Ariel if she'll take us out in her fishing boat. Then we can show him the lake."

"Below Skull Cliff!" David added. "The water's real clear there."

Claire's ponytail was swinging as she marched along the trail. "Yes!" she cried. "We might discover something interesting on the bottom!"

# The End

Get a Sneak Peek at Jeff, David, and Claire's next exciting adventure:

# The Haunting of Hillside School

## 1
## "Something's Out There"

The old schoolhouse creaked in the autumn wind. Nine-year-old Claire Posey was upstairs in her after-school pottery class when suddenly she turned to look out the window. A girl's face, pale and round, was staring in. But how could that be? The art room was high up on the second floor.

As Claire blinked, the face disappeared. Stunned, she blinked again, but all she saw were the mountains and stormy sky. When a sharp gust of wind rattled the windowpane, she rubbed her arms, shivering.

"David," she whispered to her cousin, who sat beside her at the table.

"Just a second." David Bridger was ten years old and busy shaping a submarine out of his clay. Rows of miniature torpedoes covered his math book. His blond hair hung over his eyes.

"David, something's out there. A girl. She was looking in at us."

"What?" He jumped up, knocking his chair to the floor. Hands sticky with clay, the cousins dashed to the window, followed by several other students who had heard the commotion. They all peered out. Two stories below, the ground was carpeted with golden leaves.

"Weird," said Claire. "There's no ladder or anything."

"Maybe someone climbed this tree," David said. He wiped his hands on his shirt, looking out at a tall aspen. Its branches were nearly bare, its remaining leaves fluttering in the wind. Two squirrels chased each other down its trunk, but there was no girl.

"She had dark hair, in two braids," Claire said.

Ronald McCoy pressed his goopy hands to the glass, then smooshed the clay around, creating a mess. He was Claire's age. "So what d'you see now?" he said to her. "A ghost? *Whooo, whooo*, I'm so scared. In the olden days, a girl got murdered here, so maybe she's haunting this place?—"

"Boys and girls!" called Miss Wiggins, clapping her hands for their attention. She was their art instructor and also taught ballet on Saturdays. "Return to your seats, please, and tidy up. Ronald McCoy, once again you'll be staying after class, this time to clean that window."

Claire and David wiped off their table and washed up at the sink. Long ago, Hillside School had been a mansion, and this room had been a butler's kitchen. The town of Cabin Creek was so small, and the mansion was so big, all the children from kindergarten through ninth grade were able to attend Hillside.

"Claire, let's get Jeff. Maybe he saw something, too," David said, referring to his older brother, who was downstairs at his guitar lesson. "Ready?"

"Yep," said Claire. Being practical and in a hurry, she dried her hands on the seat of her jeans instead of using a paper towel. She hefted her backpack to her shoulder. Her curly red hair was in a ponytail, which bounced as they rushed down the wide staircase. Jeff waited for them in the entry hall, neatly dressed in a sweater and collared shirt. When they told him what had happened, his brown eyes sparkled with mischief. He was twelve and always ready for adventure.

"A ghost? *Really?*" Jeff grinned. He picked up his guitar case. "Okay, then. We better start investigating."

*T*he schoolhouse cast a long shadow in the late afternoon. The cousins searched the bushes for a ladder or a scaffold. They tried finding footholds in the large stones of the building—to see if someone could have

91

climbed up—but the cracks were too narrow. And the tree's branches weren't close enough to the second-floor window for anyone to have perched.

Gazing up, they noticed a light in the art room. Ronald McCoy was cleaning the glass. When he looked down and saw the cousins, he stuck out his tongue at them.

"That window's pretty high up," Jeff said, giving Ronald a friendly wave.

"And there're no climbing ropes or pulleys," added David. "Claire, are you sure—"

"Guys, I know what I saw! It was a girl with braids. Dark hair. She was watching us." Claire zipped up her sweatshirt, stomping her feet to keep warm. Prepared as usual, she pulled mittens from her pocket and put them on.

The air was growing cold. The aspen and oak trees swished in the wind. Leaves swirled across the lawn with a noisy crackle.

Jeff looked up at the storm clouds. "Guys, let's go home. Something's giving me the creeps."

Read all of the
CABIN CREEK
MYSTERIES

Turn the page to see the
others:

# #1  THE SECRET OF ROBBER'S CAVE

Lost Island was off limits--until now.  Jeff and
David are going to the desert island to search for
clues.  And hidden treasure!  Town legend tells of
a robber and a secret cave, but the brothers have to
piece the truth together.  With the help of their
cousin, Claire, they'll get to the bottom of the
mystery, no matter what they have to dig up.

# #2  CLUE AT THE BOTTOM OF THE LAKE

It's the middle of the night when Jeff spots
someone dumping a large bundle into the lake.  It's
too dark to identify anyone--or anything.  But the
cousins immediately suspect foul play, and plunge
right into the mystery.  Before they know it, the
kids of Cabin Creek are in too deep.  Everyone is a
suspect--and the cousins are all in danger.

# #3  THE LEGEND OF SKULL CLIFF

When a camper disappears from the dangerous
lookout at Skull Cliff, the cousins wonder if it is
the old town curse at work.  Then the police
discover a ransom note, and everyone is in search
of a kidnaper.  But Jeff, David, and Claire can't

make the clues fit. Was the bossy boy from the city kidnapped, or did something even spookier take place on Skull Cliff.

## #4  THE HAUNTING OF HILLSIDE SCHOOL

When a girl's face appears, then disappears, outside a window of their spooky old schoolhouse, the cousins think they've seen a ghost. More strange clues--piano music lilting through empty halls, a secret passageway, and an old portrait that looks like the girl from the window--make Jeff, David, and Claire begin to wonder: Is their school just spooky, or could it be ... haunted?

## #5  THE BLIZZARD ON BLUE MOUNTAIN

Jeff, David, and Claire love their winter break jobs at the ski chalet on Blue Mountain, where they get to snowboard and go sledding between shifts of cleaning and tending to the grounds. But when things start going missing from the chalet, the cousins find themselves prime suspects. Can they solve the mystery before they get ski-lifted out of their winter wonderland? Or will trying to solve the case make them the frosty culprit's next target?

## #6  THE SECRET OF THE JUNKYARD SHADOW

The cousins discover a mysterious stranger sneaking into the local dump.  When bikes, toasters, and other items disappear all over town, they begin to suspect he might be up to no good.  But when these items show up again, fixed and freshly painted, Jeff, David, and Claire are confused.  What kind of thief repairs and returns his stolen goods?


## #7  THE PHANTOM OF HIDDEN HORSE RANCH

During summer vacation the cousins are excited to visit their grandparents on Hidden Horse Ranch.  They get to sleep in a bunkhouse, swim in a pond with a rope swing, and ride horses any time they want.  But they arrive to find that a mysterious fire has destroyed the stables, and the herd has escaped into the nearby canyons.  Also troubling, valuable objects have been disappearing from the ranch house.  As Jeff, David, and Claire follow clues and suspects, they keep running into dead-ends and wonder if the ranch has a phantom.

# About the Author

*K*ristiana Gregory's popular *Cabin Creek Mysteries* are from stories she told her sons where they were little and needed a bribe to go to bed. All she needed to say was, "Do you guys want to hear a Jeff and David story?" and *boom*, they were there. She is  working on her next mystery, which continues the cousins' adventures in the rugged American West.

Kristiana grew up in Manhattan Beach, California, two blocks from the ocean and has always loved to make up stories. Her first rejection letter at age eleven was for a poem she wrote in class when she was supposed to be doing a math assignment. She's had a myriad of odd jobs: telephone operator, lifeguard, camp counselor, reporter, book reviewer & columnist for the Los Angeles Times, and finally author.

*Jenny of the Tetons* (Harcourt) won the Golden Kite Award in 1989 and was the first of two-dozen historical novels for middle-grade readers.

*Bronte's Book Club* is set in a town by the sea and is inspired by her own childhood and the girls' book club she led for several years. Besides her memoir, it's her most personal work

*Nugget: The Wildest, Most Heartbreakin'est Mining Camp in the West*, takes place in an Idaho mining camp of 1866, based on the song, "My Darling Clementine." It was chosen as the Idaho book for the 2010 National Book Festival, sponsored by the Library of Congress: honorary Chairs were President Barack Obama and First Lady Michelle Obama. Kristiana's most recent title in Scholastic's Dear America series is *Cannons At Dawn*, a sequel to the best-selling *The Winter of Red Snow*, which was made into a movie for the HBO Family Channel.

Her memoir, *Longhand: One Writer's Journey* reveals behind-the-scenes of children's publishing, and the origin of ideas.

Kristiana and her husband live in Idaho with their golden retriever, Poppy. Their two adult sons visit often. In her spare time she loves to swim, hike, read, do yoga, look at clouds, and hang out with friends.

# Kristiana's Books

For a complete list please visit her website:
kristianagregory.com

Kristiana's blog:
notesfromthesunroom.blogspot.com/

Amazon page:
amazon_com_Kristiana_Gregory_e_B000APTEWK

45947432R00063

Made in the USA
Lexington, KY
17 October 2015